BRIM KIDDIES STORIES SERIES

ALIBI IN THE COT

JANE LANDEY

1

Alibi sleeps in the cot.

Alibi crawls to the door.

My little car, pipi,
Popo

Alibi's first steps.

A little duck for Alibi.

She rides a bicycle.

Draw a ball below
and color.

Father buys ice cream for Alibi.

Alibi and a boy
are on the
playground

Mother buys a doll
for Alibi.

Alibi is one year old.

Alibi can walk
about now.

Alibi can eat her food.

Alibi can sit and
watch.

Alibi can say,
mummy.

Alibi can say,
daddy.

Can you see
Alibi ride bicycle?

Can you see Alibi
drawing

Can you see Alibi
and the rainbow?

Can you see Alibi
playing with her
friends here?

Alibi is a good girl.

BRIM KIDDIES STORIES SERIES

1) ALIBI IN THE COT
2) ALIBI AND HER FRIEND
3) ALIBI AND HER PET
4) ALIBI'S FIRST DAY IN SCHOOL
5) ALIBI VISITS THE ZOO
6) ALIBI FINDS A COIN
7) ALIBI CONFESSES
8) ALIBI HAS A BROTHER
9) ALIBI AND MOTHER
10) ALIBI GROWS UP

Made in the USA
Middletown, DE
29 March 2017